PEONIES AND PERIL

A TREEHOUSE HOTEL COZY MYSTERY
(BOOK 1)

SUE HOLLOWELL

Peonies and Peril

Copyright © 2020 by Sue Hollowell

Cover design by Donna L. Rogers dlrcoverdesigns.com

Editing by: Tiffany White at Writers Untapped

CONTENTS

CHAPTER ONE

Mom kept the books for the Cedarbrook Treehouse Hotel on a shelf along one wall. There were six bookcases with stacks of grid-lined paper journals. At least she had the sense to put a date on the front of each one. Trouble was, I had no idea what the date represented. But it was a start. Mom, Brittany, and I hunkered down in the office of the hotel, attempting to excavate any sense of order to the bookkeeping for the business.

"Mom, why didn't you ever get with the twenty-first century and use a computer? These books are a mess. I can't even discern the basics of income and expenses. For example, what's 'tomorrow's baby'?"

"Chloe, you were always such a worrywart. Don't stress. I've been doing fine since Marty died and we still sometimes have guests."

"I'm not a worrywart, huh, boy?" My faithful companion looked up at me with big brown eyes.

"What was that, dear?" my mother questioned.

"Nothing, Mom. Just talking to Max."

"You and that dog. You'd think you were best friends." My gaze met Max's in perfect understanding. He shrugged, and I sighed.

My head hurt and it was only 9:00 a.m. Unraveling the mess of books for this place would take a while. It was such a beautiful place. You felt like you'd gone back in time to your childhood. Who wouldn't love staying in a treehouse? Most units had basic plumbing, some had heat. Each one was raised above the ground. You reached most places either through stairs or one even had a suspension bridge. No TVs. Each treehouse was on the edge of a central gathering area where you could have a campfire. If you closed your eyes when you were inside, you felt like you were the last person on the planet. Their names reflected local agricultural items: Crabapple Chalet, Buttercup Bungalow, Cherry Cottage, Morning Glory Manor, Snowberry Sanctuary, and Huckleberry Hut. The fact the place had deteriorated under Mom's watch was not her fault. I just hoped I could help make it financially attractive to a buyer. I like a good number puzzle, but this was a doozy. Unlike any sudoku I'd ever mastered.

"Why didn't you at least hire an accountant? I'm shocked the IRS hasn't descended and confiscated every asset you have."

"I did, Chloe. I hired Walter on Sandy's recommendation. He did the accounting for the Garden Club for a while, but he turned out to be a loser, so Edna fired him too."

I couldn't tell if the place was salvageable or if I'd have to start over. That alone diverted my brain to a huckleberry vodka. But I'd wait until at least afternoon so I didn't endure Mom's wrath. Or maybe I wouldn't. I'd get the wrath for something or other, might as well make it something I'd enjoy.

"Seriously, Mom. I don't know if I can fix this. You might just have to sell the hotel so someone with experience in these things can come in and do it the right way."

"Chloe, no! We can't sell. I'm sure you can handle it. You are an accountant, right? So we're good."

Chloe the fixer. Always the one to get everyone out of a jam. Here's an idea - don't get into the jam in the first place. The weight of returning home pressed down on my chest. I missed my own space. The distance between me and my family. My own identity, separate from these crazy people. Taking care of others had always fallen to me. I was the oldest of four kids. But only by a few minutes. My sisters Zoe, Joey, and I were triplets. No doubt we were a massive handful for Mom. I never had kids, so I can't even imagine one, let alone three at once. And if that weren't enough, baby brother Harrison came along a year later. The fact we were all alive was probably a feat in itself for Mom.

Mom had her own drama. Seven husbands. Maybe she kept going until lucky number seven. It turned out to be true. Marty was a gem. Frankly, I don't know what he saw in Mom. Four kids, six prior husbands, kind of a train wreck. But somehow they made it work. Marty seemed to get Mom. He brought out the best in her. For all of my life, her time with Marty made her the happiest. Not gonna lie, when they married I was skeptical. Mostly on Marty's behalf. I sure missed him. When he passed with no kids, the hotel became Mom's. I don't know how she kept it going for all these years.

"Brittany, do you understand the system?" I asked.

"Aunt Chloe, I just do what your Mom asks. We have these enormous books here where I write when someone makes a reservation and the amount they will pay. Then when I get a bill, I write a check and write that amount down next to it."

Heavens to mergatroyd, my head's going to explode! I took a cleansing, deep breath. *How am I ever going to get through this? And it's no good arguing with Mom. She's got her own revisionist history.*

"OK, I think I'll take the most recent book and start from the beginning. Mom, what time do you need to be at Caroline's for the Garden Club meeting?"

"Eleven o'clock."

I swear, an inch of dust covered the books. One spark and this whole place would explode in an inferno. I'd only been back a month, but it

4

seemed like I'd never left. I loved my Mom. She had a hard life and did the best she could. I knew that. But I wanted to enjoy my retirement and keep my distance for the life I'd built.

—ele—

If I could shape up this place to be more presentable, I'd only help my cause. I was a bit rusty at DIY projects, but maybe I'd have to break out my old tool belt. Frank and I had enjoyed remodeling in our spare time. I missed those times terribly with my husband. His passing was so sudden. The 1950s house we bought looked nothing like it did when we first moved in.

In the meantime, I cracked open the first book. Line one, Davenport family— $297.24. OK, that seems straightforward. Line two, Edges— $12.98. For all of my education and experience as an accountant, I'd never seen anything like this. And I'd worked for some doozies of a company. Maybe having all of this go up in flames wasn't a bad idea after all.

"Mom or Brittany, what is Edges for $12.98?"

They looked at each other and shrugged.

"Is it a company?" I asked. "Is it a product? It can't be a guest. It's too small of an amount."

"Sorry, Aunt Chloe. Doesn't ring a bell."

My phone buzzed. The sound rescued me from this accounting nightmare. Caroline was calling, saving me from the number jungle, for now.

"Hi Caroline, what's up?" Caroline was a high school friend. Pretty much everyone in this town could claim that mantle. When you grew up in a town of about two thousand, everyone was more like extended family, and they all knew your business.

"Chloe, it's Edna!" she yelled into the phone, causing me to extend it from my ear.

"What? Isn't this Caroline?" I asked. Mom and Brittany were now engrossed from hearing my side of the conversation.

"Chloe, yes. This is me, Caroline. I'm at Edna's."

"Caroline. What's happening? Are you OK?"

"I am. But Edna's not. I came by to pick her up for the Garden Club meeting. You know we're having elections today. I wanted to be nice to her because I'm sure nobody will vote to keep her president. I mean, she has that ridiculous platform to beautify the town by—"

"Caroline, what's going on?"

The rivalry between those two ran deep. All the way back to school. Always competing any way they could, especially for boys. Edna won in that category. Her boyfriend previously dated Caroline. And Edna never let Caroline forget it. Max stood. His big droopy ears swayed as he meandered over to me. He stared, imparting empathy.

"When I got here and rang the bell, there was no answer. The front door was open and just the screen door was closed. I yelled for Edna. Because, you know, she's so private I didn't want to just barge in."

"Caroline, spit it out. What's going on?"

"Edna's dead." I looked at Mom, not wanting to repeat what I just heard.

"How do you know? Where is she?"

Mom, Brittany, and Max were all now on alert that something was not right at the other end of that phone line.

"Oh, Chloe." Caroline blubbered so hard I couldn't understand a word. I needed her to calm down without alarming everyone else and creating a panic I couldn't control.

"Caroline. Breathe and tell me where she is."

"Chloe, what's happening?" Mom now joined the panic party. "Is Edna all right? Chloe!"

"Chloe, she's facedown in her garden. It looks like she's just sleeping. I yelled at her and shook her and no response. I touched her." Caroline lost it and sobbed so hard I figured we were done. Plus, I got the gist.

"Caroline, is Ralph there?" Silence. "Caroline. Listen to me." She mumbled something close enough to concurrence. "Go inside the house, drink some water, and sit down. We'll be there soon. Can you do that?" More mumbling.

I disconnected the call. Mom and Brittany sprang up. Max sprinted toward the door. Road trip to Edna's. And another opportunity to hang his head out the window where his long fur blew like he was Farrah Fawcett at a photo shoot. Well, this wasn't the diversion I would have asked for from my accounting job of a lifetime. I had to admit, Spokane wasn't dull, but it was my life, my choices. Somehow in Cedarbrook, drama swirled like tornadoes on a regular basis, sweeping up everyone in its path. No life untouched. It was barely 9:30 a.m. on a Monday. If deciphering the hotel books wasn't enough of a puzzle to solve, now we had a death.

CHAPTER TWO

T he drive to Edna's took about ten minutes. Every trip in this town took about ten minutes.

"Chloe, are you going to tell me what's going on?" Mom asked.

I couldn't keep it quiet much longer. She'd figure it out when we arrived and saw Edna splayed in her back yard.

"Caroline said something's wrong with Edna. She got there and couldn't find her, so she went to her garden."

"Did she have a heart attack? I knew it. I kept telling her not eat so much of that red meat. It seemed like every day she was at that Smokehouse Restaurant scarfing down steak. I knew it'd get her. Wait 'til I give her a piece of my mind. She never listened when I was married to her dad, either." Lloyd was Edna's dad, Mom's husband number three. She tried to mother Edna as a teenager and that didn't go well.

I had to let the cat out of the bag before we got there. Caroline was hysterical enough. I couldn't be outnumbered with runaway emotions. Even with Max the Calmer by my side, it'd still be too much to tackle.

"Mom, it looks like Edna's dead."

She gave me a pointed look. "Chloe, stop joking. I'm sure Caroline was just being dramatic. Or you misunderstood. You know Caroline and Edna both want to be Garden Club president. And we're having the election today. Caroline will do anything to oust Edna. She's never gotten over the defeat."

"Mom, I'm serious. Caroline said she found her face down in her backyard," I whispered.

Saying it any louder felt like it would make it come true. I glanced at Mom in the front passenger seat. Her face stoic. That woman had seen a fair amount of death in her lifetime, more than most.

"But, Chloe. It can't be. Maybe she just fell and passed out."

I pulled into the cul-de-sac, circling counterclockwise to park on the street just before Edna's house. Caroline's Cadillac filled the driveway. Mom sprang from the car with the energy of someone forty years her junior. Physically, she was still in pretty amazing shape. Mentally she was obviously aging. Max and I quickly exited and caught up with her. Edna's dog Trixie barked with the veracity of a Doberman. That little Cavalier King Charles spaniel was too adorable to harm a fly.

"Mom, hang on. Let's go find Caroline first."

She complied.

We approached the screen door and I could see through it that Caroline had followed my instructions. The door squeaked as I slowly pushed it aside. Mom and Max followed me in. The door slammed behind us and jolted Caroline. Her head snapped in our direction with tears streaked down her face.

"Oh, Mabel. I can't believe she's gone. Poor Edna," Caroline moaned.

Max pushed his way to the front and rested his head on Caroline's knee. She lifted a hand from the water glass and placed it on his head. No tail wagging for now. Somehow, he knew this was not a happy visit. Trixie mirrored his actions and sat by his side with her head on Caroline's foot.

"Mom, you stay here with Caroline." Further obedience without a peep. I left the both of them in Max's capable paws and headed to a bedroom to find a blanket. I pulled the comforter off of a bed in the spare room and used the hallway through the kitchen to the backyard.

Yep, there she was.

Face down in her prized peonies. I gently covered her as if she were taking an afternoon nap. I'd never seen a dead body up close and personal. Frank had relayed stories from his time on the force, but there was nothing like a front row seat.

"Hi, Chloe." I jumped, almost falling myself.

Max and Trixie sped around the yard, figurines falling like dominoes. They stopped to observe and sniff Edna. And after a quick pit stop, resumed their romping and chasing crows. I shuffled them safely back inside.

"Sorry, should have shut the door," said Buzz, who I'd called before I left the hotel.

"It's OK, Buzz. We're all understandably distracted. Sorry to bother you on the golf course." Buzz was a retired cop from our town. But today, I was thankful he agreed to come.

"Where's Ralph?" Buzz asked.

"He went to pick up car parts in Emerald Hills."

"Oh yeah. The Studebaker's gone." Buzz worked his way along the garden path, winding past the yard art, figurines and jungle of flowers and shrubs. "Dang, I really hoped someone was mistaken. Or at least pulling my leg, as cruel a joke that would be."

Sunflowers were everywhere, as if seeds had been sprayed from a hose. They were pretty cute but didn't seem to fit the design and tone of the fancier garden. Edna's garden was one of her prized possessions. She won awards every year for many of her flowers. The hotel sure could have used her touch with designing beautiful garden spaces.

"I'm afraid not. I wonder what happened. Mom said Edna's diet could have caused a heart attack, maybe that's it."

Buzz circled the body, an experienced law enforcement officer keenly eying clues.

"Not sure. It looks like she possibly tripped over something. But that shouldn't cause a death by itself. Some of the peonies appear trampled. And these morning glory vines look like they could reach out and trip you. What is that glass ball over there?"

Buzz referred to a gazing globe that normally would have been situated on a display stand. The blue-swirled orb now sat shattered about eight feet from Edna's head, the stand on its side.

"That's a gazing globe, a garden decoration."

"A what?" Buzz knelt down and examined the pieces of the globe. "You ladies and your garden things. Well, maybe she tripped on the vines and hit her head on it. I see a bump the size of a golf ball near her ear."

"Buzz, what do we do now?"

"I'll call over to Emerald Hills PD and have them take it from here. Hmmph."

"Buzz, what are you thinking? This was an accident, right?"

Buzz and I went way back. It had been over forty years since I'd spent any real time with him. We were such confidants back then, sharing our dreams and our woes. When we dated in high school, that nonverbal communication style drove me nuts. I was a very concrete person. Just say what you're thinking and not all of those other guttural sounds I was supposed to translate.

"Well, Chloe. I think so. But frankly, from the position she's laying, the tripping and hitting her head don't line up with the truth. Just best to have the pros take a gander."

This was horrible. Edna wasn't the most likable person, but her death would send shock waves through the town. I headed inside to see what mess I'd have to clean up there.

Max and Trixie had returned to their duty station at Caroline's side. Thankfully, they followed directions, unlike Mom. She was nowhere to be found. I searched the house to no avail. Maybe she returned to the car, not wanting to be anywhere near death. I headed to the driveway. She was on the phone, pacing. She spotted me and gave a little wave.

"Mom, we need to go."

She stopped in her tracks and stared at me.

"Mom!" That earned me a dirty look. She had a handful of tissues stopping up her tears and sniffles.

"You know, Pearl, I didn't like her either, but I'd certainly never wish her dead. I mean Edna was such a pill when I was married to her father. But I did have a soft spot for her too. Pearl, I have to go. I'll see you in a bit." She hung up the phone.

I planted my hands on my hips. "What are you doing talking to Pearl? I hope you didn't tell her what's going on. We need to leave that to the authorities. It's not our place."

"Chloe, are you kidding me?" Mom shook her head and stomped toward me. "Of course I called Pearl. First of all, she's Buzz's wife so she'll know soon enough anyway. Plus, I wanted her to know we need to find another person to run against Caroline for the Garden Club president and wanted to see if maybe she would do it. I mean, just because Edna's gone doesn't mean Caroline should get the position free and clear."

You always chose a side in this town. And Mom was definitely on Team Edna.

"Mom, I'm sure that's the last thing on Caroline's mind right now. I'm going back inside to get the dogs and we'll head back to the hotel. I'm sure by now Brittany could use some help."

She followed my return to the house and through the slamming screen door. Buzz had joined Caroline. She hadn't moved a muscle. Max and Trixie stood guard as if Caroline was president and they were the secret service. I searched the kitchen and utility room to gather Trixie's food, leash, and dog bed. When I returned to the living room, Mom sat next to Caroline with her hand on her back, consoling her.

"Chloe, I called the Emerald Hills guys," Buzz said. "They're on their way. I'll wait here so you guys can go."

"Chloe," my mom said. "We can't leave until we find out what happened to Edna. Why don't you stay here and help? I'll go with Caroline to the Garden Club meeting."

We froze.

"Yes, Mabel's right." Caroline had come out of her stupor and back to the conscious world. "I think having the election would be what Edna would have wanted."

"I agree, Caroline." Mom gave me a sharp look. "Besides, Chloe. You're one of the smartest people I know. I mean, you're helping me straighten out the books at the hotel. That's kind of like being a detective, in a way."

Now she'd really lost it. "That's ridiculous. I'd just be in the way. The pros have this handled. Besides, I need to take care of the dogs." A quick glance down showed Trixie and Max patiently waiting for my next move.

"Well, look how well-behaved they are. They'll be fine with us. You don't mind them coming to your store, do you, Caroline?"

I was pretty sure with the way Caroline's mouth turned to a frown that she did mind. But her diversion of the election gave her a free and clear path to become the Garden Club president.

I shook my head. "I'm not staying. But Buzz? Can you give me a call later with an update?"

That appeased Mom. Pretty sure this day couldn't get worse. Digging through those hotel financial journals, and poor Edna's death. The story was that she was a gruff, difficult woman to deal with. She didn't have it easy growing up. Her Mom left her when she was young. Over time, her behavior resembled the classic eccentric old woman. She wouldn't harm a fly but was the kind of person that gave off a vibe you either liked or you didn't. People didn't understand what Ralph saw in her. Beauty was in the eye of the beholder. I truly believed there was someone on the planet to love every person. Edna wasn't afraid to speak her mind. That got her into some hefty disagreements on a regular basis. I really hoped that had nothing to do with her death.

"Plus, we have an election to conduct," Caroline mumbled to herself as she zipped out the door and sped away from the quiet cul-de-sac.

Did Caroline seriously just say that? How could she even think of having the Garden Club election today?

Mom didn't seem to notice as she led us silently out of the house, with me and the dogs bringing up the rear. Max and Trixie bounced along as they saw they were going for a ride. I wished my outlook could change on a dime like a dog's does. One minute extremely somber, then the next, prancing down the walk for that ultimate road trip. I held the back door of my car open. The dogs bounded in. I tossed Trixie's supplies in the back and we headed to Caroline's. What new uproar was in store for us there?

CHAPTER THREE

Max and Trixie jockeyed for the open spot to see through to the front seat. "Knock it off, you two. Good manners or I'll take you home." Right. Max had me wrapped around his puppy paw since I had adopted him at six weeks. My rescue Cocker Spaniel had the sensitivity of a psychic and seemed to know my thoughts and feelings before I did. He melted my heart with his compassionate, large brown, warm eyes. His buff-colored, long fur, and droopy ears exuded a regal look. Trixie was a whole other story. She was like the pesky little sister. A stinker, but cute as a bug. Her chestnut and white body wiggled even more wildly than Max's did when she wagged her tail.

We pulled into the small parking lot at Caroline's Confections. The two-story building looked the same as the day it was built in the 1950s. The brick-lined flowerbed that hugged the building held sad little multi-colored geraniums. How could a member of the Garden

Club accept that with a straight face? Especially one who wanted to be president of those wacky women? Caroline rented out the upper floor to a young couple for additional income.

"Mom, wait here while I get the dogs' leashes." I got out of the car and went to the back, where they both just about leapt out of the car before I slammed the hatch.

"Chloe, why don't you go back to the hotel? I can call you when we're done."

With the pups leading the way and straining my arm, I entered the store. "I'm fine, Mom. Let's just see how it goes."

"Don't say I didn't warn you."

Mom and I wound our way through the loads of stuff Caroline had for sale. One might call it crap. Her coffee shop had turned into a hodgepodge where the confections seemed to be an afterthought. It was as if any old idea about what to sell made its way into this place. We navigated through the miniature doll display, the hanging plants, and the hat rack, to an opening behind the bakery counter. A small room with tables, chairs, and no windows had become the meeting place for the Garden Club. Initially, Caroline had offered the space for free, but now charged a small fee for its use. She was running a business, not a charity. I heard the chatter before we entered the room. Max had stopped to smell a tray of gingerbread cookies cooling on a side table. His sweet tooth ruled him again. He sat on his haunches and gazed at me for approval. *Not now, buddy.* I gently tugged and we went into the room.

Caroline was holding court. The place was full, and it wasn't even time for the meeting to start. I heard low mumbles and Edna's name. In a town of this size, when you sneeze, the people on the other side of the street say 'bless you'. Literally nothing was a secret. The more you tried to keep something on the down low, the more likely it got out.

"Caroline, you must be traumatized after seeing that," Sandy said. She was forever trying to get into Caroline's good graces. From the dawn of time, Sandy attempted entry into Caroline's clique. For a time, Caroline would temporarily admit her, only to shun her.

"Oh, Sandy. I can't even begin to tell you how horrible it was," Caroline moaned. "And poor Edna was up for Garden Club president re-election. And there she was, lying dead in her own garden. Well, maybe that was a fitting way for her to go." Gasps echoed throughout the room. Mom sniffed.

"I bet she ate some of those peonies," Loretta said, wiping her eyes. "She was always making those salads with her flowers and she probably mistook the poison ones. Did the cops say what happened?"

"Let's not speculate," I said. "We need to wait for the medical examiner's report." All heads turned toward me, Mom, and the dogs. The four of us joined a table in the corner.

"Hi Chloe, so nice to see you. Hi Mabel. Is that Edna's dog?" Sandy asked.

"Yes, for now I'm keeping her. She'll be a nice playmate for Max until we find her a new home. I know Ralph never wanted her in the first place."

Trixie yipped. Sandy jumped. "Well, keep her away from me. She seems vicious. Every time I was at Edna's she mauled me."

Trixie yipped again. *I agree, girl. Sandy can be a lot to take in.* Max sidled next to Trixie, his stubby tail pointed straight back, ears cocked forward. His demeanor confirmed suspicions that Sandy was not a dog person. And why would she be at Edna's? She didn't even like her.

"Wait," Sandy continued. "What if it wasn't an accident after all?"

"Whoa." I raised my hands. "Please, let's wait for the report. I'll call Buzz to get an update and you'll all be the first to know." Give 'em what they want. First in line for gossip.

"Well, maybe I should just talk to Buzz myself, then," Sandy snipped. She wouldn't let this go. "You know, Edna and Ralph argued all the time. He's such a hothead. The last time they were at the Smokehouse, they were going at it again."

"About what? Where is he anyway?" Loretta chimed in.

"Chloe's right." All heads swiveled toward Caroline. "Let's wait for the authorities to do their thing and we'll get on with our meeting. I mean, I'm sure Edna would want us to carry on with the election. You all know how important this club was to her."

Some heads nodded. More mumbles disagreed about proceeding.

Max and Trixie settled on the floor, watching the goings on like a tennis match. Eyes darted from one speaker to the next, ready to bound when anyone made a move. Caroline stood and went to the podium. The dogs jumped to attention. Max's ears lurched forward again. His instinct for people was spot on and he sensed something about Caroline wasn't quite what it seemed. He peeked an eye toward me, ensuring I was fully aware of the concern.

"On behalf of Edna," Caroline said, "I'd like to call the meeting to order."

"Caroline, I just think it's shameful of us to carry on as if nothing has happened," Mom said. "Shouldn't we wait an appropriate amount of time? Chloe, how much time should we wait after someone dies before we have our meeting?"

"Mom, I don't know. We're all here. And there's nothing we can do right now. I agree with Caroline. Edna would have wanted us to carry on. She cared a lot about the work this group does."

Caroline grinned, appearing confident in her victory.

CHAPTER FOUR

The packed house sat in rapt attention. This would be the talk of the town for the foreseeable future. An unexplained death and the gall to proceed with an election that same day.

"I couldn't agree more, Chloe. OK. First order of business is reading of last meeting's minutes." Caroline behaved as if she'd already been elected. "Loretta, would you please do the honors? And seriously, we need to elect an official secretary and treasurer. The willy-nilly record keeping of Edna's was atrocious. Who knows what shape the club is really in? When she fired Walter, that was the last straw for me." Caroline was in full-on campaigning mode. "I just can't." Loretta sniffled. "It's too soon. We're dishonoring Edna. I don't know how you can stand up there as if nothing has happened. It's heartless." Loretta continued into a blubber.

"She's right, Caroline." Pearl patted Loretta's back, joining Team Edna. "Let's postpone for a week. At least until we say a proper good-bye to Edna."

Max lifted his head and squinted intensely at me. His eyes inquired about the rising tension in the room. I reached over and gave him a reassuring pat. Trixie stood, inching as close to Max as possible, and plopped her body right on top of him. As if to say, you pet him, you must pet me too. What a diva. He tipped his head down toward her and raised his eyebrows. *Really, girl?*

"Chloe's logic makes sense. How about we have the election and then close the meeting early?" Caroline wouldn't let this go until she had her way. "I'd like to share my plans for the club. Then if anyone else wants to get into the running for the position, you can go next." Without the boldness of Edna, I had no idea who'd be brave enough to challenge Caroline.

"Well, I guess I could," Pearl said.

Caroline's shoulders deflated. I'm sure she had hoped for an un-contested election. Likely with Edna as an opponent she wouldn't have won. "OK. Here we go." Caroline gripped the podium with both hands like she was trying to keep it from toppling over. Her knuckles whitened.

"Ladies of the Garden Club." She was going all out with a show. Drama in this little club rivaled a Broadway production. "I'd like to share with you today my plans to take the work we do to new heights. To make this club the envy of the county. To make more money than we ever have in the past." There it was. Caroline's focus never strayed far from the almighty buck. Her family had owned the bakery for many years. But it looked exactly the same as it had for generations. There were more things for sale than bakery items, making me question what business she was really in. If she had such a brilliant business mind, why had the place continued to look as if it would fall apart any day? Rumors swirled about financial troubles. Caroline finished her stump speech, paused, and took in the smattering of claps. She took a seat in the front row, a smug smile on her face, as Pearl made her way to the podium. Pearl would be a great president. From a business perspective, she appeared to have it much more together than Caroline. Pearl's Pooch Pampering was a thriving business, even in this tiny town. People spent a ton of money on their dogs. She had customers from all over the county.

"First, let me say, I wouldn't be doing this if Edna were still alive. I really just want to be able to carry on her legacy. We are a garden club and Edna was all about the plants. Sure, we made some money and we need that to operate. But first and foremost, I believe our agricultural focus should remain, just as Edna would have wanted." Pearl nailed it.

I didn't know she had this in her. Despite her reluctance to pursue the position I was sure she'd sway some votes to her side.

"That's right, Pearl," Mom cheered her on.

"Mom," I whispered.

"What?" she replied. "Pearl's right."

"Mabel, let her finish. Then we can take our vote." Caroline huffed and rolled her eyes.

"I think that's all I need to say. Thank you." A similar smattering of claps for Pearl sounded throughout the room.

Caroline leapt to the podium, resuming charge. Low chatter began at each table. "OK, everyone. Now it's time to vote. At each table are pens and slips of paper. Write down your vote and put your paper in the box up here. Chloe, we need a neutral party to count the votes. Would you do that?"

I'd hoped to be a fly on the wall here. But now I was smack dab in the center. "Sure. Mom, can you hold the leashes to keep these two in check?"

One by one, each Garden Club member approached the ballot box and deposited her vote. If Caroline didn't win, we'd hear no end to it. For that reason alone, I cared just that much for her to be the victor. Sandy was the last to cast her vote. Averting her eyes, she took her seat. The room full of women was eerily silent. I took a piece of paper and pen from the podium to tally the votes. I made two columns and labeled each with the name of the candidate. I opened the box and set the top aside. I retrieved the first, a folded piece of paper.

"One vote for Pearl." I entered a tally mark in Pearl's column. I retrieved paper number two, slowly and obviously for all to see. "One vote for Pearl." Another tally mark. From the corner of my eye, I could see Caroline in the front row slump just a little in her seat. She was probably counting bodies in the room to calculate the number to win. I retrieved another ballot. "One vote for Caroline." She raised back up to a full-seated height. There were eight more votes, the total an odd number. We'd have a winner today. I continued my announcements, adding votes neck and neck for Pearl and Caroline. Ten counted, one to go. I looked in the box to confirm the final piece of paper. "The last vote goes to—" I swear I heard a gasp. "Caroline. Congratulations."

She flew out of her seat and to the podium in two steps, nudging me aside with a snide look. I returned to my table and was greeted like royalty from the pups. Unconditional love.

"Well, as your new president we have lots of work to do. First off—"

"Wait, I thought we were postponing any business until after the election to—" Loretta interjected.

"What I was trying to say before the interruption is that I think we should honor Edna in some way." Caroline forged ahead as if she'd been waiting for this moment forever. "I have lots of ideas. What I want to do is name a scholarship after her for students who will study agriculture in college."

"I think that's something we should vote on," Sandy said. Caroline's ally questioned her actions. If looks could kill, we'd have two dead club members. Yikes! This wasn't just for fun, it was serious business.

"We don't need a vote." Caroline glared at her. "Let's just do it. I mean, who could dispute that it represents Edna well?"

No one wanted to argue, so Caroline achieved her second triumph in a mere ten minutes. Silence enveloped the room. Caroline gaveled the meeting to an end, the sound echoing. I led the way with the pups to escape the awkwardness and stifling air closing in. I couldn't get out of there fast enough. *Note to self. Next time, just drop Mom off at the meeting.*

CHAPTER FIVE

M om and I had stopped for coffee before joining Brittany at the hotel for another day digging into the hotel books. I was so torn about staying at Mom's during my visit. With my plan to only be here six months or so, it didn't make sense to get my own place. Mom, Max, Trixie, and I arrived early to continue the scavenger hunt for a glimmer of organization in how the hotel operated. I didn't fault Mom. How would she know any different? And Brittany helped as much as possible. But neither of them had the education or experience to successfully run this place. Or heck, even just to keep it afloat. If I could make heads or tails about the books, I might be able to convince a buyer to take over. It was such a bummer it had gone downhill.

I tapped my pen against the thick book. "Mom, let's see if we can get the most recent books organized today. Let's focus on just the previous month." I'd give her the fact she tracked items in the log, but any sort of system? Not even close. "Brittany, I'm thinking if we had a white board in here, we could use that as we work through each item. Left column expenses, right column revenue. Would you be able to go the office supply story in Emerald Hills and pick that up?"

"Sure, Aunt Chloe. Anything else?"

"Do you have cleaning supplies here? I want it to look as nice as possible when guests come. We need repeat business and some good reviews to boost the desirability."

"Chloe, it gives it a rustic charm." Mom sat in the corner, flipping through her magazine. "You know in the olden days they didn't have maids like you had at your house. You shouldn't criticize it. We get a lot of compliments on how authentic the place is."

I seriously doubted that. But a dust rag once in a while wouldn't hurt. I looked over at the dogs and saw Trixie's white coat looking more like charcoal and chestnut with no hint of white. Max had cleared out a spot on the floor and his nose was covered in dust bunnies. I took a deep breath to gather my thoughts. It was easy to criticize. I'd work on building Mom up. I didn't know how much more time we had together, and I needed to make the most of it.

"More coffee, Brittany," I said. "I'm afraid to plug in that coffee maker."

Brittany stood. "Yeah, we've had smoke coming out of it from time to time."

"Would you want to take the pups with you for a road trip? I think they're going to get antsy staying here for too long."

"Sure, c'mon, guys. Let's go on a ride." Brittany waved them through the door.

Trixie leapt up and body-checked Max. He paused, letting her take the lead. I worried Trixie's assertive ways would further push Max into his shell. I'd need to keep an eye on her to make sure she didn't bully him. He was my number one. When that bossy little girl entered the picture, he probably wondered who was this thing rocking his world?

"OK, Mom. While we're waiting for Brittany to get our supplies, let's start organizing these binders." I pushed all of the tables into a row so we could line up the books in what I hoped was some semblance of chronological order. There was one small window to the side of the room. It did little to lighten the place. I moved a lamp closer to our work area, which didn't provide much more light beyond what you might see in a rustic cabin with no electricity. I should have added a lamp to Brittany's shopping list. Or ten lamps. Onward. Mom and I lugged six of the binders to the table. I opened the first one, and dust flew.

"Mom, do you have any blank or unused books? I think I might have to start fresh with some of these."

"Of course, Chloe. I'm not totally incompetent." She brought two large notebooks to the table and dropped them next to me. Another cloud of dust rose up. When she came in, Brittany would be hard-pressed to see us, cloaked in this shroud. I sure hoped the pups didn't have an issue with the dust.

"Mom, it looks like this binder starts with January of this year. Let's go through that. Maybe the more recent ones will be easier to remember."

Mom shrugged. "Whatever you say, Chloe. You're the expert."

"We need this as orderly as possible to attract a buyer."

"Oh, Chloe. I can't sell. This is Marty's legacy. He'd roll over in his grave. I just need you to get it organized and then I can take it from there. I'm sure you'll do better than that incompetent accountant. I wish I'd never hired him. Even I could tell he was a dunce with the numbers."

I hoped I could live up to her expectations. The place had so much potential. Back in the day, it was booked solid, a real destination hotel. It had become a kind of community hub with fun events and outdoor adventures year-round.

"We'll just need to make a best guess for what's in the books." I sat in the chair with the book on my lap. "Let's see if we can get through one book a day." At least that was a start to piece together this puzzle. "January second, Pete's Plumbing. OK. That's a great start. Do you remember where you had plumbing work done?" Max's eyebrows twitched as if I was on the right path.

"Of course. It was that persnickety Snowberry Sanctuary. Having a hot tub in that unit is such a pain. There's always one problem or another with it."

The Snowberry Sanctuary was our highest-end rental. It was the largest at nine hundred square feet. The territorial view felt like you were on top of the world. If you didn't know better, you'd think you were in a four-star hotel room. It was also the place that required the most work and was rented the least of any of the treehouses. After getting these books together, we needed to seriously consider decommissioning that unit. Or at least simplifying it for maintenance purposes.

"What's this second entry? It just says 'Joey' for five hundred dollars."

"Your sister always needs money for rent or bailing someone out of jail. You know, she doesn't make very much working at that restaurant. And at her age, she shouldn't be a waitress. But what else can she do?"

"Mom, you can't use the business money for personal use. Is it just this one time or is there more?"

Mom waved her hand in the air. "You know Joey. She's always got some emergency or another."

"I'm going to get a second notebook to write down personal expenses. Can we agree from now on you don't pay personal items from the business account?"

"You're the expert," she said for the second time. "I'll do what you say. I wish Joey was more like you. Then I wouldn't have to keep rescuing her. I'm so glad you're here." Mom reached across the table for my hand. "I mean, with you helping solve Edna's death. I'm sure you'll be able to figure it out. You're really good at those number puzzles. What are they?"

"Sudoku." I was pretty good, regularly solving at least the hard level. If you worked it enough, you eventually figured it out. There was always an answer, you just had to be persistent and try different options. Max and I teamed up on those, sometimes setting a timer to see how fast we could get the answers.

"Plus, you were married to a cop. So you probably picked up a lot from that about detective work."

"Mom, let's just keep to the task at hand." I flipped through a few more books, skimming. "Reconstructing these books is going to take all of my time and energy. I told you I'm only here for six months to help you through this so the hotel can be listed for sale. I have my own life away from here."

Mom sighed. "I know. But it would be so nice to have my family together again. We could really use you here to help with Joey. She has all those kids and grandkids. I can't even keep track there's so many now. We'd only need Harrison to move back so we could all be like it was before. I mean, how could my only son leave his mom like that?"

Harrison had followed my path and beat feet out of town as soon as he'd finished school.

"Let's keep going on the books." The next couple of entries looked pretty straightforward. Thank heaven for that. *Good job, Mom.*

"Chloe, doesn't that sound nice? We were such a happy family when we were all together. I want that again before I die. I don't know how much more time I have."

Oh boy. Guilt trip commenced. Buckle up for a ride down the well-worn path. Mom tried hard, but her choices fell short. She always felt as if she should have a husband. Mostly, for someone to help with the kids. But who wants a ready-made family? That's a big reason I have Max. He knows what I'm thinking and totally gets me. When I need a pick-me-up, he grins as wide as a Muppet and wags his stubby little tail to make me grin. It works every time.

CHAPTER SIX

Buzz had a good thing going with his barber shop. The exterior had a quaint, inviting look with the classic barber pole and a large, square window that took up most of the front wall bordering the sidewalk. He had a little flag posted out front, reading *Now Open*. The door was propped open to let in a lovely, cool breeze. Buzz had a recliner brought in to use when he wasn't working. His feet propped up with a newspaper draped across his midsection.

"Hi, Buzz."

He twitched, faking as if I didn't wake him from a slumber.

"Hey, Chloe. C'mon in." He lowered the footrest of the recliner, crumpled the paper, and plopped it onto a side table. "I was just catching up on the news."

It boggled my mind how this town managed to keep a local newspaper going.

"Thanks. I'm just checking in on any progress in Edna's death. You know I'm not going to get a moment's peace at home until this is solved. And frankly, I need all the energy I have to keep going through the books at the hotel."

"Yeah, that's gotta be somethin'. I hope you get it sorted out."

"Maybe you could come help? I sure could use your detective skills. It's a real head-scratcher for most of what I'm finding."

Buzz chuckled, his belly jiggling up and down.

"Well, this thing with Edna is about all I can do. There's a reason I retired from the force and took up snipping hair. I don't usually have to haul people off to jail at the end of the appointment." He laughed at his own joke. His middle jiggled again.

I took a seat in the only guest chair in the place.

"You know it. Perks of retirement. That men's club, though. More drama than a high school play. But that's a story for another day. You'll have to dust off your clubs and play a round while you're still here."

"Brilliant idea. I need to get out of the house and that dingy hotel. I have a sinking feeling that even after all the time I spend getting the books in order, we won't be able to find a buyer. If only Mom considered selling when it was still doing well."

"So I talked with the boys in Emerald Hills. They've got to be the ones to handle this."

"Any update yet on cause of death? Edna wasn't a young chick. But Mom has her suspicions of something nefarious. You know how it is once the gossip train leaves the station and gains some steam."

"Pretty much. There's no stopping it. You just have to wait until a new topic comes up and then it's off to the races again. It's so nice having you back, Chloe. Even if it's just for a short time."

Buzz was a good guy. I thought so in high school and he'd maintained that 'til now. We'd dated for a year before I left. We had really enjoyed our time together, but it was clear we'd never be more than just friends. I'd left on good terms. "Yeah, you know why I can't stay."

"I know. But maybe there's a way you can come back and maintain your own identity. Your independence from your family. You shouldn't have to feel compelled to rescue them anymore. And Harrison isn't even in town." Buzz had been my confidant in those years before I moved away. He knew the nitty-gritty of what I'd had to do to manage the household when Mom wasn't there.

"I'll think about it. But I don't see it happening. So what's the verdict from the Emerald Hills guys? What do they have so far?"

"Can we keep this between us for now?" Buzz's tone was ominous.

"Um, OK. You've got me worried, Buzz."

"Well, there's several things that appear questionable. Until they can rule them out, we don't need to fuel the fire."

"Like what?" I got up and stood against the wall.

"Right now, they're looking into how she got a bump on her head."

I gasped. "Buzz, what are they thinking?"

"Chloe, one step at a time. It could be anything. She could have tripped and hit her head on something. You know how that little Trixie of hers was always underfoot."

"Indeed. That girl is clingy. And she's quite the pest to Max. What else?" I paced, wondering how I'd keep a straight face when I got home. I needed a cover story to hold off Mom's grilling.

"Those morning glory vines were everywhere. She may have tripped on those. That gazing globe was off its stand, in pieces. Really, Chloe, we could speculate all day long. We've got to establish some facts and data before we get too far."

"The Garden Club yesterday had this wild idea." I thought Buzz was going to lose it.

He doubled over and slapped his knee.

"That's a statement of the obvious. Do tell. What's the latest from the ladies?"

I didn't want to say. It was pretty far-fetched. But you had to rule things out too. "They think she ate some poisonous flowers by mistake." There. The cockamamie idea was now out there.

Buzz was silent. He rubbed his chin. He looked at me, then got out of the chair, went to the mini-fridge, and got a bottle of beer. He snapped off the top and handed it to me. I was tempted but shook my head. He took a long swig, draining about half the bottle. He wiped his mouth with his hand and returned to the chair.

"Chloe, I'm trying to discount that for every reason I can think of. But that might not be as crazy as it sounds. On the one hand, she was a master gardener, winning all of those awards. On the other hand, she did make all of those dishes with edible flowers. Could she have inadvertently mixed them up?"

"I don't want to make this worse, Buzz. But I think we should be looking at everything."

"*We?* Now I have a partner?"

"Well, Mom's more upset than she's letting on. I need this resolved for her. I'll do what I can. I mean, I did learn a thing or two from Frank during all those years he was on the force."

Buzz frowned. "Patience, Chloe. Let's get that round of golf on the books. See what you got after all these years."

"Sounds good, Buzz. It's great to catch up with you. I better scoot. Gotta make sure the house is still in one piece. I'm more worried about Mom than the dogs. And I need some rest for another day excavating those hotel books."

Buzz got up and we hugged. I was thankful for this calm, bright spot in my day. I was headed back to the hotel to see what mayhem had ensued with my absence.

CHAPTER SEVEN

Trixie busted through the door first, seemingly more energy than when she left. Max trailed behind with Brittany to avoid getting in Trixie's line of fire. She wiggled her body all the way across the room for a greeting from Mom, who ignored her. She made some sort of low gurgle noise to get attention and retreated a step, still wiggling beyond belief. No acknowledgment from Mom brought a higher-pitched rumble from her and another step back. She continued this until she was at a total ear-piercing bark.

Mom cracked a smile and relented.

"OK, girl. I hear you." She scratched Trixie behind the ears with both hands. Serenity for a moment. Trixie moved on to me, like we were the royal receiving party. I quickly gave her the ear scratch as well.

Brittany made eye contact with me to assess the situation. I shrugged a bit. "Thank you so much for getting our supplies. Especially the java." I retrieved the carrier with three beverages, and she returned to her car for the remaining items. "Mom, let's take a break and have some coffee. I can only look at those for so long before my brain starts to fog up."

"It's not that bad, Chloe. You could stand to be more positive and not complain so much." I bit my tongue. Maybe she was right.

Brittany returned. "Aunt Chloe, where do you want these? I got three of them." She lugged the first whiteboard inside.

I moved a table closer to the wall and propped it up so we could all see it. Brittany left the room to retrieve the remaining items. I wasn't sure using these would help much, but it would allow us to better organize the materials and maybe speed up the process. A small puff of dust rose from an overstuffed chair as Mom retrieved her coffee and took a seat. The chair faced away from our work area, as if Mom was in time out.

"Brittany, thank you so much for running the errand. I hope having the pups with you wasn't too much trouble."

Trixie settled on the fleece throw that I had when I first adopted Max. Like everything of his, she'd claimed it as her own in a matter of a day.

Max, the gentleman, stood next to her pondering his next move. He acquiesced and plopped onto the floor, one paw on the blanket. A message of peace but not full surrender. My sweet, sweet boy. *I'm sorry she's totally turned your life upside down. It's just for now, boy. I'll figure something out soon.*

"Nah, they were great," Brittany said. "I put both of them in the back, but Trixie insisted she be in the front seat. I think that was better for Max too. She kept pushing him to the side so she could see out the front."

Max looked at me to confirm the account. Brittany patted him on the head. Trixie bolted up, intervened, and almost toppled Max. He stumbled, and seeing his opportunity, tiptoed around her to take a seat on the blanket. Oblivious, Trixie usurped Brittany's attention.

"Well, thanks again, Britt. We're taking a coffee break, then back at it. I set this up to try and have a system to go through the books from this year as a start."

Trixie turned and spotted Max on the blanket. She stood right next to him and flung her body practically on top of him. He raised his head and pleaded for help. He couldn't have looked less comfortable but wouldn't yield an inch. I'd have to be more thoughtful about each of them having enough of everything.

"Oh, smart, Aunt Chloe. That'll make it easier to remember some of the stuff. I'll help however I can."

Mom sipped her coffee, giving me the silent treatment. I really did need to find a way to get along with her.

"Chloe, why don't we do a big family dinner?" she asked, coming back to the conversation. "I would love to have my daughters back together again."

I looked at Brittany and paused before my reply. *Be the bigger person, Chloe.* "OK, Mom. I'll have to figure out when I have time."

"Chloe, you make time for family." She rose from the chair and returned to the work area. "Oh, this will be great. You girls back together. Too bad Harrison moved away. You know, he hardly ever calls me."

My baby brother had the same idea when he graduated from high school. He didn't have a destination, but instead packed up his car with everything he had and just started driving east. Maybe I'd reach out to him again and let him know what was going on with Mom. He might want one last chance to mend the relationship. No matter what happened, she was our mom.

"Sounds good, Mom."

"Fabulous! I'll start the planning." She got a notebook and started jotting ideas down.

I took a sip of my coffee. "Mom, we've got a lot of work to do here. I need you to help."

"Oh, Brittany can do that. She knows as much as I do about what's going on."

I looked at Brittany. She gave a small nod yes. That was probably just as well. I wondered if all this was for naught, or would I be successful in my mission?

CHAPTER EIGHT

Brittany and I had finished our coffee. "OK, Britt. Let's see if we can get through January and February by lunch time. It's a lot. But if we don't get hung up on every minuscule detail, I think we can do it."

"Sure thing."

Max came over and assumed the position he always held when we solved our puzzles. He raised his paw and placed it at my elbow. He rested his snout on the book to help me with the clues. "We just started January and got through about the first week." I turned the page of the notebook and dust flew. I scratched my nose and rubbed my eyes. This place could use a good vacuum.

We worked through week two of January. Brittany did have a better memory recall, so this went more smoothly. Some legit expenses, some of Mom's shenanigans. *That's OK. It's a starting point to improve upon.*

"Great job, Brittany. Let's do week three." We started to get into a rhythm. The more recent entries were a piece of cake. I was petrified of finishing this and going back to prior years. I'd save that for later. Maybe we could get away with not doing that for now. I opened another book and more dust emerged. Max sneezed and shook his head to clear it out. Trixie glared at the nerve of him to disturb her peace. He looked at me and gave a big grin.

A loud ring startled the dogs so much that Trixie jumped up and yelped. Her face looked perplexed like she wondered who dared disturb the princess with that obnoxious noise. Max stood and watched the Trixie show. Danger, schmanger.

Mom hadn't replaced the office phone yet with a cell phone. It rang the old-fashioned ring. I felt like I'd need to ask Ernestine to patch me through. I reached the source of Trixie's annoyance and answered the phone. She ceased barking. "Cedarbrook Treehouse Hotel. Chloe speaking. How can I help you?"

Mom's nose was still buried in the family reunion planning notebook, oblivious to a customer calling.

"Hi, Arthur. What can I do for you?"

Mom looked inquisitively at me. I shrugged my shoulders. It was a short conversation, and when I finished, I hung up the phone.

"Edna had a nephew?" I had no idea. But I'd been gone so long I wasn't in the know.

"Not that I know of," Mom said.

"Me neither," Brittany said.

"Well that guy, Arthur, said he was her nephew. He lives in Oklahoma. He called over to Edna's and whoever answered the phone told him to call me and tell him what happened. Not sure how I landed smack dab in the middle of this." The more I tried to keep arm's length of anything going on in this town, the more I got sucked in. It was a vortex of histrionics with no escape.

"What did he want?" Mom asked.

"Not exactly sure. Except he quizzed me about where Edna's stuff would end up. He didn't even express any sympathy or ask about a service for her." What was his angle? I wasn't aware of any relatives who might inherit her estate. Her boyfriend Ralph wouldn't be the one since they'd never married.

"So, Chloe. We'll have to drive out to Zoe's to invite her to the family dinner. I think she lives so far away without a phone so she doesn't have to call or see me. And Joey works at the restaurant, so that's an easy one. I don't think she'll ever leave that place. I mean, what else could she do? She never went to college like you did, Chloe."

Oh, Mom. "Well, we have a lot to do here. So it won't be anytime soon." I needed to focus on getting these books in order. Second,

48

spending time fixing it up could prove fruitful. I had some rookie knowledge of repairs from the projects Frank and I had completed. "Mom, what do you think about sprucing up around here? I think we could do some things to make it look pretty good. I might as well take advantage of my time here. I've got some ideas for decorating and getting the grounds shaped up."

"That sounds great, Chloe. Maybe I could bring some of my garden gnomes to cheer it up." Hmm. Maybe. Max looked up at me and questioned that suggestion too. Those little creatures probably wigged him out as much as they did me. He was eye level with them. Maybe we could put them in their own little section.

Brittany and I resumed our rhythm of review. We'd gotten through January and were into February. Thankfully, there were a few patterns I spotted and some repeated entries, making it a bit easier to decipher. Why did Arthur's phone call bother me? I couldn't put a finger on it. I'd met selfish people all my life. Maybe he was in shock. Since I didn't know him, maybe he didn't come across as caring in general. Nope, not that. I did not have a good feeling about him.

CHAPTER NINE

"Good morning, Mom." Trixie and Max had already been up, outside for play, had breakfast, and were lounging next to me on the patio. With that rest, they were eager for another playmate. But it wouldn't be Mom. They took off on a race around the yard.

"Chloe, can you keep those dogs quiet?" Mom shuffled her slippered feet through the patio door to the kitchen. "I just got up and I haven't even had coffee yet. Look what they're doing, knocking things over."

I needed to corral them or we'd have an incident on our hands. I noticed one of Mom's cherished gnomes in her set of *See No Evil, Hear No Evil, Speak No Evil* had been knocked over. I'd have to set it back up or she'd have a fit.

"Max. Trixie. Time to go inside." They stopped in their tracks and pleaded for more romp time. "Sorry guys, we'll play more later." They followed me inside. Trixie, of course, had taken over Max's larger bed. Only the best for the princess. Max had squeezed his body into Trixie's smaller bed, looking like Goldilocks in Baby Bear's bed. Good enough for now. I couldn't have my sensitive boy's feelings hurt. He would always be my number one.

Mom ambled back into the dining room, her hair a bird's nest, her light pink fluffy robe cinched tight around her waist. She'd had that ratty thing as long as I could remember. She plopped into the seat across from me and let out a noisy sigh. I didn't bite.

"Mom, Buzz and I are heading to Edna's this morning for a bit. We're going to meet Detective Jansen from Emerald Hills to look over things. It appears Edna's death is suspicious."

Mom perked up as if she'd had three cups of coffee. "Oooo, Chloe. I knew it. Call me right after that. I have to know what happens."

Uh, no. She could wait until I got home. One word to her and the town crier would have the news blasted before I even returned.

"I doubt I'll know anything more. I'm heading out in a bit. I'm going to take just Max this time and give him a break from Trixie. Then, I'll be back to get you and head to the hotel."

"That's fine. She's not too bad when she's by herself."

I think she secretly liked the company. Last night before bed, Trixie had snuggled up next to Mom on the couch, and they looked like they'd been made for each other.

—eee—

I pulled up to Edna's house within a few minutes of leaving home. The detective's car was parked parallel to the house. Buzz's car was in the driveway. Thankfully, we'd have a chance to talk details without being interrupted. I parked behind the detective's car and headed into the house. My stomach was unsure if it was upset over the breakfast I ate or the thought of entering a deceased person's home. I opened the screen door and entered. The old lady smell was just as it was the day we found Edna. I followed the sound of voices to the garden. Buzz and the detective stood just outside the sliding door.

"Hi, Chloe," Buzz said. "We waited for you. This is Detective Jansen from the Emerald Hill's office.

Rudy, this is Chloe. One of my dear friends from yesteryear." Buzz and his belly jiggled at the funny. Rudy and I shook hands. He was taller than Buzz, but most everyone was. His hair had thinned on top and the sides grayed just a touch. Distinguished, as they say about men when their aging shows.

"Nice to meet you. Not sure how I can help. Where's Ralph? I saw the Studebaker, but his other car's gone."

"He let us in, then went to do some errands. I think it's all still too fresh for him."

"We're just surveying the scene right now. The preliminary autopsy report indicated a large contusion on the right rear of her head. We're trying to piece together a scenario that could explain that. She was face down. If she'd fallen and then hit her head, the contusion would likely be on the front, or even the side. But not the back. Let's go to where she fell and see what the view looks like from there."

Edna's garden was magazine-worthy. She manicured every bush, tree, and flower for a picture-perfect scene. The winding brick paths led around bird baths, waterfalls, and several garden gnomes. I didn't know what people saw in those odd little creatures. Both her and Mom had taken up collecting the kooky ceramics. It had become a competition between the two as to who had the better collection. Edna had the same set as Mom. Although her *Speak No Evil* was missing. Max had wandered off the path to the set, noticing the absence of the third gnome. The fact it was gone, an oddity. We wound our way through to the location where Edna's body had been found.

"So I'm going to stand in the spot where Edna's feet were when she fell," the detective said. "Let's see what that perspective brings for any further explanation." Buzz and I remained a few steps back. "OK, from here I can see the stand where the gazing globe had been. But it's nowhere near her, so I don't see how she could have fallen onto it."

We stood there, soaking in the picture, willing it to speak some answers.

"Those morning glory vines are covering part of the walkway. Could she have tripped on those?" Buzz asked.

"Possibly," Detective Jansen said. "We've got a couple of key questions to answer. That's one of them. The other is how did she get the contusion?"

"Her dog could also have made her stumble. She's small and gets underfoot at times," I said.

"Possibly." He pressed his lips into a thin line.

He kept things close to the vest. They probably teach you that in detective school. Never share details with a civilian.

"I'm going to make some drawings before I go," the detective continued. "Sometimes, letting these things percolate can help guide you to the answers." He took out a sketchpad and pencil and started drawing. He walked ten feet to the right side where Edna's head had faced, turned around and drew some more. He continued viewing the scene from all angles to complete his picture. "Thank you both for your help. I'll be in touch."

I was actually thankful he hadn't shared much. That way I could truthfully tell Mom I didn't know. We silently retraced our steps through the garden and house to the driveway. We all shook hands and said we'd look forward to an update. I got in my car and headed home to gather Mom.

Max looked at me and whimpered. "I know, boy. This is our biggest puzzle yet to solve. Good job noticing that gnome was missing." Who could possibly want to hurt Edna? Frank was suspiciously absent at just the right time. And Caroline found her. Was the Garden Club presidency that big of a deal to her reputation?

CHAPTER TEN

M om, the pups, and I had eaten lunch at home and been at the office about an hour. We were getting into a rhythm of reviewing her books and deciphering the entries. Our success rate was about 50 percent, guessing the entry correctly or giving up and putting it into a *we gave it our best shot* bucket.

"So, Chloe. When we go visit Zoe later, don't be shocked by what you see. I mean she's living the hippie lifestyle, not a care in the world."

"Thanks for the heads-up, Mom." I had no idea what to expect. Zoe lived with her boyfriend of many years, off-grid. In a way, that sounded wonderful. That type of living fit my criteria for being independent and having my own identity.

"I mean, she doesn't even have a phone to call her. How backwoods is that? Even I'm up with the times and have a cell phone." She was so not up with the times. Case in point: the hotel bookkeeping.

I looked forward to seeing Zoe. The previous times I had visited Cedarbrook it was a crap shoot whether I'd see her or not. She kept to herself but was friendly when we got together. I'd never been to her place. We'd always met at Mom's, and that never gave us much of a chance to talk freely.

Mom licked her thumb and flipped a page of the book in front of her. "It's going to be so great when we all get together for our dinner."

It was going to be something. Great was a stretch. I'd take civil.

"I'm looking forward to it. I wanted to make sure to see Zoe and Joey before I leave." I kept reiterating my plans to keep them on Mom's radar. She talked as if I had come back for good. Not even close. Six months was a huge commitment to stay and help prepare the hotel for sale. The main thing keeping my sanity was knowing there was an end date to my term.

"Chloe, I just know after our dinner you'll want to stay. It will be great to have my daughters together again before I die. I'll be so happy."

The door to the office opened, letting in much needed light. If I stayed in town, and Mom retained the hotel, there was a growing list of upgrades I wanted to make. A new window or two in the office was one of them. I looked up, fully expecting to see Brittany. I did a double take since the person had long brown hair like my niece. The individual entering, however, was taller and a little heavier than Britt.

He held the door open, as if pondering his decision to fully enter the room.

"Can I help you?" I asked.

"Yes, I'd like to rent one of your treehouses, if you have one available."

I sat stunned, not sure if I'd heard correctly. We actually had a customer.

"I'm sorry?" I said, wanting to confirm what I understood.

"Do you not have any available?"

"Oh no, we do." I scrambled to meet him at the desk we used for checking in. Mom followed. She stood behind me with her arms folded as she assessed the young man, with his long hair, baggy jeans, and sloppy plaid shirt. "We have a few choices of cabins for you. Do you have any specific requests?"

"We need a deposit first," Mom blurted.

I closed my eyes for a second.

"What she means is that we'll need a credit card for the reservation. But we won't charge you until you leave."

"That's not what I mean," Mom continued. "We can't have people coming in, thinking they can stiff us. So we need to be paid up front."

Wow! No wonder the place felt like a ghost town; she had the most unwelcoming attitude.

"It's OK." He shrugged. "I have cash."

Max nonchalantly strolled over and stood right next to me. He was so close I felt a low rumble from his body. He looked up at me to affirm his displeasure with this guest. *I know, boy. Something doesn't seem right with me either.*

I opened the reservation book and handed him a card to fill out. "Great. Let's get you registered, then I'll take you to the Huckleberry Hut." As long as I was here, we'd have great customer service. Huckleberry Hut was one of our more basic units. The size resembled a standard hotel room. It was also currently the cleanest, bedding laundered and room dusted, waiting for a guest.

Mom hadn't budged, her arms wrapped tight around her in skepticism.

"That sounds nice," the man said.

Huckleberry Hut was one of the few cabins with most everything working. The heater was kaput. But since the weather was warmer that wasn't an immediate issue. I just hoped he thought it was nice when he actually saw the place. He filled out the registration card and I took his money for the first night.

"How long will you be staying with us?" I asked.

"Not sure. Just needed a getaway from the rat race for a few days." I nodded. "What do you recommend for a restaurant?"

"There's not much in town. Nothing you'd like." Mom couldn't have tried harder to deter him from staying.

Well, this explained why the hotel wasn't profitable. "There's the Smokehouse Restaurant for a nice sit down meal. And a little deli or a burger place for to-go items."

"You probably won't like them." Mom continued her rant.

We were saved by the interruption of Brittany arriving in the office. Thankfully she'd been visiting each cabin to make sure they weren't in total disarray from critters or some such thing.

"Hi Britt. Would you please take our new guest to the Huckleberry Hut?" I grabbed the dusty key from the wall hook, nonchalantly wiping the grime from it before handing it to Brittany.

"Sure thing. Right this way."

The door closed and I wheeled around. "You could be nicer to the guests. They're the only glimmer we have of keeping this place afloat to attract a decent buyer." Max walked over to Mom, tilted his head, and arched an eyebrow. He seemed to be taking her side.

"He's going to stiff us. I can tell his type. If you had more experience here, Chloe, you'd be able to tell that too." She returned to her chair at our worktable.

"What's his *type*, Mom? Paying customer?" I couldn't help myself. My mouth and my brain were not in sync. I inhaled through my chest and diaphragm, holding my breath for five seconds and slowly letting it out.

"Mark my words, Chloe. A sloppy guy dressed like your hippie sister is bad news. I've been doing this long enough that I've seen it all. And he smelled like the pot. We don't need druggies here."

A little part of me wondered that too. But no chance I'd give her the satisfaction of agreeing before it actually happened. I'd wait and see. Hope for the best.

"When Brittany gets back to hold down the fort, let's head out to Zoe's." My strategy to change the subject when Mom went down a rathole with her negative comments usually worked. I looked at the calendar and counted the number of days until I returned home. My own home.

"You're right." Mom stood. "We should go soon. It's so far out in the boonies it takes forever to get there. I'll never know why they felt the need to build a house a million miles away."

I left it at that.

CHAPTER ELEVEN

M om was right about the boonies. I was pretty sure we'd been in the car an hour and hadn't seen a house in a while. Talk about separation. Thankfully, I'd looked at the GPS ahead of time and an overhead map. That gave me a general sense of direction we were headed. The thick forest made everything look identical. Passing mile marker thirty-two was the landmark I was looking for. A lightly graveled, mostly dirt road led into the grove of trees. We began our trek down the pothole lined route for who knows how long. The gullies were so deep the dogs bounced in the back seat like they were on a trampoline. Walking from here might have been a better plan, but I had no idea how much farther we had to go. I slowed as much as I could but still kept the momentum.

"You were right, Mom. This couldn't be more secluded if they tried."

"You always were the most responsible and logical one. If only you'd stayed in town, maybe Zoe and Joey could have had your positive influence. When you were taking care of things at home, everything was so much better."

We continued bounding down the path, Mom's small stature a benefit so she didn't carom off the roof as we descended some of the holes.

She gazed out the window, in her own reality. "At least we always had a roof over our heads, and food and clothes." She sniffled. Her voice cracked.

"I'm just glad that somehow you found Marty. He was such a gem. His kindness was all that you deserve, Mom." She extracted a tissue from her purse and blew her nose. "Do you know about how much longer before we're there?"

"How do I know, Chloe?"

The pups had settled into the seat, figuring that if they hugged it they'd be better than ricocheting off the ceiling. Max was off to the side, Trixie hogging the middle view. I couldn't wait to reward them with a romp around the place when we arrived. I'm sure they could use the stress relief too. We must have traveled for at least another ten minutes before the sky lightened above. Max stood and caught my eye in the rear-view mirror. He grinned wide. I couldn't resist that smooshy face, ever. I matched his smile, my spirits instantly perked. His tail wiggled in response.

"Mom, I'm sorry about Edna. I know you two had your moments in the past. But I see that her death is hitting you hard."

She continued her gaze out the window.

"I'm surprised about it, myself," Mom said. "She was such a snot most of the time when I was married to Lloyd. She was a spoiled-rotten daddy's girl. Got everything she wanted. She could do no wrong in Lloyd's eyes. I think that was one of the reasons we got divorced."

"That must have been a sad time for you." All of her kids were out of the house when she'd married Lloyd. I'm sure the empty nest feeling contributed to her loneliness. From four kids in the zoo to zero kids and deathly quiet. I know after Frank passed, the quiet ate away at my brain. My mind aimlessly wandered to some not so happy places. Mom had always lived with another person, and when Lloyd left it probably broke her heart. I needed to find some answers about Edna so Mom had some peace.

"Yeah, it was. I always wondered if I could have done something differently. I tried to get along with Edna, but she created wedges between Lloyd and me on a regular basis. I think to spite me, she kept that beautiful antique ring he promised to me. She'd wear it around and flaunt it. I guess to prove to herself that she won the love competition of her father."

This was probably the most vulnerable my mom had ever been with me. For the remainder of my time in town, I'd prioritize encouraging. Everyone deserved happiness.

"It looks like we might be there." I hit the last pothole and launched into a wide open space. I saw the cutest little log house and what must have been a barn. At least ten sheep inhabited a corral. I spotted pigs and chickens and a vegetable garden that could have fed an army. I have to say, it wasn't what I expected. I pulled up to the house entryway and parked. Trixie let loose with a thundering yip like she was escaping a long stint in prison. She scrambled to the front seat and squirted out my door as I opened it. Max looked at me, requesting permission. He had better manners than most people I knew. I nodded and he followed Trixie's path to freedom. I circled the car to help Mom out. I reached my hand to support her exit and she waved it off.

"I can do it, Chloe. I'm not a cripple, you know." I withdrew my hand and held the door. She hoisted herself out, steadied on her feet, and marched off toward the front door. The dogs, enamored with the animals, watched the other creatures as if at a zoo.

Zoe emerged from the house as we approached. "Hello," she greeted. *Let the games begin.*

CHAPTER TWELVE

Her smile as wide as the open space on the property, Zoe had aged beautifully. Her long, flowing silver hair cascaded behind her. Her arms were outstretched for a warm hug, her multi-colored three-fourths length skirt a testament to her wild side.

"Hi, Chloe. You look amazing. Retirement agrees with you." My sister embraced me long and hard. She released and continued to hold my hand. Looking deeply into my eyes, she said, "I was so sorry to hear about Frank."

"Thank you."

"Can we go inside?" Mom wrinkled her nose. "It stinks out here."

"Of course, Mom. I made some raspberry scones to go with our tea." Zoe squeezed my hand and led the way into the house.

"Max, Trixie." They stopped in their tracks, incredulous I'd interrupt nirvana. Reluctantly, my boy obeyed. Begrudgingly, Trixie followed. They followed Zoe inside and collapsed on the floor, panting, tongues extended.

It was a beautiful log cabin that Zoe and her boyfriend had milled out of logs from their own property. The surrounding landscape had natural growth that showed loving care. What they had built for themselves was impressive and quite an accomplishment. I would love to use their expertise to enhance the hotel. With their eye to beautify using nature, they could do wonders for making it more attractive.

The inside of the house was just as comfortable, a sanctuary in itself. The furniture was also built from wood on their property. We entered the kitchen and sat at the table. A platter filled with scones sat center place. A teapot on the stove began to warm for our accompanying beverages.

"It still smells like a pig sty in here. I don't know how you stand it, Zoe. I don't think I can eat with that smell. It's making me nauseous."

Zoe angled away from Mom toward me. "So Chloe, tell me how things are going with the hotel."

"We're making good progress going through the books. I'm hopeful we can get those in shape and then get a realtor to list it for sale. My goal is to be back home before winter."

"Chloe, you know I don't want to sell the place." Mom crossed her arms. "I just needed your help to get it up and running in good shape again. Then I can take it back over. Zoe, can you talk some sense into her moving back home? I still never understood why you girls moved so far away from home." Mom scoffed. "Can I just get a glass of water?"

Zoe rose from the table and went to the refrigerator to get a pitcher of filtered water. She poured a glass of crystal clear liquid. She set it in front of Mom who raised it up and examined it like a specimen. "Is this from your water barrel?"

"Yes, Mom. It's from our rain catchment system. It's perfectly fine to drink. We filter it so the taste is actually very good."

Mom set the glass down in front of her. "No thanks."

I put one of the scones on a serving plate as Zoe prepared our tea. "Mom, do you want tea? The water is boiled, further removing the impurities."

She raised her nose in the air. "I guess that would be OK. I need to use the restroom. That drive is so long out here. Do you still have that outhouse toilet?"

"It's a composting toilet, Mom. And yes, we still have that. Just do your business and I'll take care of the rest."

Mom harrumphed off to the bathroom. When she was out of earshot, Zoe said, "Chloe, you're a saint for coming to help her with the hotel. I'm really hoping she sells that place. It's too much for her and there's no way she can run it on her own. But then what would she do with her time?"

"Well," I said, "probably more of what she does now. Gossip and garage sales. Her collection of garden gnomes is insane. It's taken over her yard and moved into the house. And I find it especially creepy. But to each his own."

Zoe sat down at the table. "Chloe, are you really leaving after the hotel is listed for sale?"

"I have to, Zoe. You understand why."

"I know how it was all of those years ago. Some things are the same, but not everything. If you moved back, you could have the relationship with Mom on your terms. Be clear about your boundaries and hold to them. No guilt, no shame. I'd sure love to see you more often too. Heck, you could even come stay with us however long you needed for a break. You know Max would relish living the life of a sheepdog." Right on cue, Max sauntered over, his tongue lolled out of his mouth, taking Zoe's side.

"See? He's totally on board."

I imagined the thought of staying here, just my boy and me. Zoe could sweet talk with the best of them. She made a good case, lots of merits.

"I don't know, Zoe. It'd be such a big change for me after all this time."

"Just think about it, OK?"

I consented so that we ended this conversation before Mom returned to the room. I loved the allure of the nature and privacy.

"Zoe, why can't you live like a normal person? I mean, this backwoods stuff is ridiculous. You can't even have a proper hairdo. Look at Chloe's beautiful hair. It's nice and neat even though it's fake blonde. With all of the money I gave you, I'd think you would have a better house and better clothes."

Mom tapped the side of her teacup. "Chloe, tell your sister how you're helping solve Edna's murder."

"Mom, we don't know how she died yet. It could have been an accident." If I let on about my suspicions of murder, I wouldn't be able to get that genie back in the bottle.

"You know, she was always arguing with Ralph. It was either money or her jealousy about his prior relationship with Caroline. I think he had something to do with it, just to shut her up." Mom's theories just kept on coming. "Zoe, we're having a family dinner so you have to come."

"Of course, Mom. Just let me know when and what I can bring. We'll be there."

"Well, Eldon doesn't have to come. This is just for family." Until Zoe and Eldon married, Mom would never consider him part of the family, and likely never would. I think she blamed him for taking Zoe away from her.

I stood. "We should get going. We've got a long drive back and I'm going to check on Ralph later today to see how he's doing. Even if they fought a lot, he's still grieving." Mom grabbed her purse and beelined for the door like the place was on fire.

"Great," she said over her shoulder. "Grill him good. And let me know what he says. I never liked him, anyway."

CHAPTER THIRTEEN

I pulled into the driveway at Ralph and Edna's house. I felt bad that Ralph didn't have much help to take care of Edna's affairs, so I wanted to see if there was anything I could do to support him. Plus, I wanted time alone with him to learn more about these conflicts with Edna. Almost everyone had strife in relationships. But mostly they're in private. I brought just my boy along for this trip, giving him some relief from Trixie. Mom should have been able to handle just one dog. I turned off the car and looked at Max. His head lifted, preparing for our visit. A somber expression, knowing this was not playtime.

"Let's get your leash attached and head in."

Max stood obediently and I hooked his collar. I opened my door and he leapt across my lap and out, eager to get going to our destination.

We approached the screen door, the interior door open. I knocked. "Ralph, it's Chloe."

After about two minutes, when I was just about to give up, Ralph appeared at the door. "Sorry, Chloe. I didn't hear you. I was in the bedroom."

"No worries."

Max and I entered, and I gave Ralph a hug while Max hugged my leg. I reached down to pat him and assure him.

Ralph turned and walked down the hallway. "Come on into the kitchen where we can talk."

Max and I followed him on the route that would have taken us to the backyard. It must be excruciating to stay in the home where your loved one passed away.

"Have a seat." Ralph gestured to the dining table, then took the chair at the head of the table.

I took the place to Ralph's left. Max ventured away into the kitchen. He sat as still as a statue with his nose pointed to the countertop.

"Ralph, I'm so sorry for your loss. I'd like to help in any way I can. If you need someone to go through Edna's things at some point, I'm here for you." I peered at Max, who hadn't budged. I guess as long as he wasn't destroying anything, it was OK.

"Thanks, that would be great. There's definitely a lot of paperwork. And a lot of her personal things. I'll let you know when the time is right."

Ralph's shoulders slumped over, and there were bags under his eyes. He must have still been in shock. I think we all were.

"Sorry if I'm nosy." I leaned forward. "Did Edna have any underlying health conditions? Mom suspects her heart may have given out." Max now gave a whimper so light I almost didn't hear it. I ignored the interruption to our conversation.

Ralph shook his head. "No, not really. I just can't figure out how this happened. I really want some answers."

Max now doubled the volume of his whine.

"Ralph, I know the cops will ask this too, if they haven't already. You weren't home when Caroline came over to take her to the Garden Club and found her?"

Another whimper from Max. I glared at him to be quiet.

"No, I was buying parts for the old Studebaker. I wanted to have it running well for the car show coming up in Emerald Hills. I know the person closest to the victim is always a suspect. That hurts even more."

Was there a way to confirm his alibi? Max pierced the air with a yip. With that, I got up to bring him back to the dining room. On the kitchen counter I spied a box of gingersnaps labeled *Caroline's Confections*.

Ralph chuckled when he saw the focus of Max's attention. "Your boy sure does have a sweet tooth."

No doubt about that. Ginger seemed to be his preference. I'd learned after last Christmas that I had to locate my gingerbread men even farther out of reach than I thought. I still remember Max returning to the living room after what I thought was him going to get a drink of water or some kibble. Instead, his breath smelled of gingerbread. I went into the kitchen, and darned if one of the little guys wasn't missing and not a crumb of evidence remained, except his ginger-smelling breath.

"You don't know the half of it."

I looked at my dog. *I don't know, Max.* Why would Ralph have a box of Caroline's gingerbread cookies? Was she over here for some reason? Was there a spark being rekindled? Even before Edna's death? Did Ralph and Edna's fighting cause him to seek comfort from someone else?

I called Max over to sit next to me. Message received.

I shifted in my chair. "I'm sorry if I'm the bearer of news, but I think you should know, there's lots of gossip going around about public disagreements between you and Edna. That's fueling the fire of speculation that maybe you had something to do with her death." I let that big, ugly statement sit right there out in the open. I hoped with my open-ended statements I'd get him to keep talking.

"I know," Ralph said. "I wish we hadn't done it in public, but sometimes my temper gets the best of me. Especially when I learned she'd been taken advantage of. I was trying to protect her, but she was so fiercely independent. And the stubborn woman would never admit when she was wrong."

He was on a roll now. If Max could be patient just a bit longer, he'd be in for a real treat later. I needed to follow this line of questioning through to its conclusion.

"Who took advantage of her?"

Ralph looked out the window, pausing before his answer. It took him so long to start talking again I thought this might be the end of the line.

"It was some supposedly long-lost nephew of hers asking for money. At first, she sent him a one-time, small amount. Then it became ongoing. I thought she was being scammed. I was convinced he was taking advantage of her, and I wanted her to stop sending the money. Her big heart couldn't bear cutting him off, so she kept doing it. Then, one day she told me she discontinued the payments. I never knew why, but I was proud of her for setting boundaries." His hands had migrated to his lap. Out of the corner of my eye I saw them clenching and unclenching. Poor guy, enough grilling for now. Max and I had some work to do to put together the pieces of this puzzle. I felt like I was leaving with more questions than answers.

CHAPTER FOURTEEN

"**M**om, I'm going to be in the back during the meeting, continuing the review of the books."

"OK, Chloe. And keep those unruly dogs under wraps. I don't know why you have to bring them everywhere with us. They don't behave and they smell." Mom headed to the front of the room to sit with her friend Loretta and wait for the Garden Club meeting to start. I was pretty sure the main reason Mom was a member was for the gossip factor. It had become her hobby. Today's meeting agenda was to plan the fundraiser for the year. At the election, Caroline overran everyone into naming a scholarship in Edna's name. A nice idea, but it really should have been voted on. The ladies began to gather in the room and join their cliques. If I closed my eyes, I'd swear I was in a middle school lunchroom.

"Welcome, club members." Caroline sounded very official and quite full of herself. "Please settle in and we'll get started in a minute. I'll gavel the meeting to order when we're ready."

Since I wouldn't be around to see it all, I'd no doubt continue getting play-by-plays from Mom on our calls.

"I've got some pastries from the shop here for everyone," Caroline continued.

Mom and Loretta glanced at each other again. "Do we have to pay for them?" Loretta asked.

"No, silly. The club dues cover the costs," Caroline said. Another glance between Mom and Loretta.

"Don't you think we should vote on where we spend money?" Loretta asked. "I mean, it's nice to have the treats, but we don't have a lot of money to spend. And maybe it could better be used elsewhere." Loretta continued her challenge of Caroline.

"Well, I was just trying to do something nice. Brighten the mood for everyone after the somber meeting we had last time."

Sandy sprang to Caroline's defense. "It's not that much. And Caroline's right. It's nice to have the treats for us."

"Sure. More money in her pocket. But nothing to show for the club," Pearl chimed in.

"This isn't about money, Pearl. I'd think you would know me by now," Caroline said. "I'm going to call the meeting to order and get past this nonsense." She slammed the gavel so hard I thought the head was going to fly off. The sound startled the pups enough for them to jump up to attention, ready for the intruder.

What was behind Caroline's defensiveness? Was she really in as much debt as the rumors indicated? The minutes of the last meeting were read. Caroline's color returned and she beamed at the recap of her victorious election.

Emboldened, she continued. "The main thing for us today is to decide on the fundraising plan. We decided last time some of the money would go to a scholarship in Edna's name toward a student planning to study agriculture."

Silence from the crowd. Everyone seemed worn out from all the pregame activities.

"Who has ideas?" Caroline continued.

"I think we should do the plant sale," Loretta said. "It's always brought in good money in the past. And plants are what the club's all about." Loretta bravely forged ahead.

"Sure." Caroline tapped her chin. "That worked OK. But we need to think bigger. What's going to maximize our revenue? I'm thinking we expand what we're selling to other items." Caroline barreled on.

"Caroline," Loretta said, "we need to stay true to our mission. Agriculture. I say we stick with the plants."

"Stop thinking small. This is about honoring Edna and providing for the kids." Caroline countered.

Nobody bought that line. Something else was going on.

I tried my best to bury my nose in the hotel books. But the tension in the room was palpable. I'd have to return to them later. The meeting continued with volleys back and forth on the fundraising plan until Caroline wore everyone down. Plants plus a lot of other items that had nothing to do with plants. Caroline gaveled the meeting to a close, looking smug with another victory. No doubt they'd make more money with her plan. But it did dilute their purpose.

The ladies milled about in their cliques, whispering.

"You know, I think she just wants more money to funnel into her business." Loretta loaded a handful of gingersnaps into her purse. "I hear it isn't doing well. I mean, charging us for pastries. That's tacky. We paid for these, ladies. Be sure to get your fair share."

The whisper was loud enough for Caroline to hear, and she belted out, "How dare you! My business is doing very well."

Loretta raised her nose in the air. "I doubt it. You used to have full cases of products. Now you're lucky if you have ten percent. And adding all that other crap for sale in your shop. You're obviously in trouble."

I was pretty sure Loretta hit the nail on the head. The place looked rundown, neglected, and more like a swap meet.

"Mom, let's go."

Trixie and Max stood at attention ready to leave. We all wanted out of this mess. It was a no-win situation.

"Just a minute, Chloe. You and the dogs can go. I'll be out soon."

No way she'd miss a minute of the action.

"So what if I added to my store? It's a good business decision," Caroline said.

"Be honest for once, Caroline," Loretta said. "Pretty sure it won't kill you. And we can all see the truth anyway. Who knows? Maybe you offed Edna so you could take her place and use the money from the Garden Club to save your business."

"Yeah, or maybe you thought you could get Ralph back with Edna out of the picture," Pearl added.

That cracked Caroline open. Tears formed and dropped onto her cheek. She slumped. "I had nothing to do with Edna's death. And I resent you implying I did just to save my business."

"Well, it was you that found her. Just sayin'." Loretta was not backing down. I don't know if she believed it. But she was out to hurt.

Caroline advanced to blubbering. Sandy handed her a tissue. "I can't believe you suspect me of something so horrific. Yes, my business is struggling. I admit that. But I would never have harmed Edna. It was probably that stupid dog of hers that made her trip and hit her head." Sandy continued consoling her. As we passed by, I overheard Sandy whisper to Caroline, "No one knows more than I do how hard you work for this club and the sacrifices you've made. The sacrifices we've *both* made so you can win."

"Never mind that, Sandy. You just don't understand."

Sandy looked like the bride left at the altar. Caroline grabbed the remainder of the pastries and stormed out the door. Without a word, we all exited the room, filing out through store. From the corner of my eye, I spotted Caroline returning the unused pastries to the sales display case. How bad was her debt for the business that she had to recycle food?

CHAPTER FIFTEEN

I was not looking forward to today. Edna's memorial service was scheduled for the Shady Acres Cemetery. It was a small, overgrown place in town that would probably have given Edna a fit if she realized she was going to be there. The grass was usually a foot high, unless there was a service planned. Mom and I had a relatively silent morning, unlike most since I'd arrived. I think Edna's death had emphasized her mortality even more, putting it front and center. She was scared and today would stress her out. I prepped for an unusually high amount of snark. We left the pups at home and headed to the service. The silence continued. I pulled into the parking lot at the cemetery next to a few other cars that had arrived.

We left the car and headed toward the service location. Still not a peep from Mom. I'd just leave her to her thoughts for now. I was so pleased that, despite Edna's gruff exterior, someone had taken care to provide her with a beautiful presentation of those garden flowers that she loved. Several chairs had been placed in rows. Mom led us to the front at the left end. Even in her grief, she didn't want to miss a beat of gossip. I hoped even those who weren't the best of friends with Edna would still pay their respects. She was owed that. In continued silence, the remainder of the chairs filled in. About ten minutes after noon, the preacher approached the front of the group and began the service. Mom grabbed my hand and squeezed tight. I returned the gesture. Thankfully, I'd brought a large supply of tissues as Mom's sniffles had already begun. The preacher's words were kind, as they always were when we looked back at someone's life.

Out of the corner of my eye, I spotted motion in the parking lot. A late arrival disturbed the solemn ceremony. I didn't recognize the person. It was a younger man who made his way to the back row of chairs and took a seat on the end. Mom's sniffles flowed a steady stream. Not that I wanted her to suffer, but perhaps this reminder of an imminent death would soften her disposition, even just a little. She leaned over and whispered, "Who is that guy?"

Not wanting to disturb anyone, I turned to her and shrugged. She turned around, got a better look at him, and returned my shrug. Oh, well. Fodder for gossip at another time. I was shocked. Mom knew everyone and everything going on in town but didn't recognize the man. Odd.

The preacher finished up. Mom sniffled a final time and deposited the tissue into her purse. We held hands throughout the entire service. She got up and led me toward the car. "Now I'll never get that ring her father promised me." Even in her grief, she couldn't let it go that Edna kept the ring.

The plan was for all of us to go to Caroline's after the service. I hoped the sting of accusation had lessened since the fundraiser planning meeting. But nothing ever died down in this place. It only amped up. We arrived at the passenger door of my car and Mom let go of my hand.

"Chloe, that guy who was late looked familiar. But I don't know who it is."

I opened the door and Mom got in, then I went around and got in the driver's side.

"Not sure. I don't know many people here anymore."

I started the car and we headed to Caroline's. I just prayed the gathering didn't devolve into a gossip-fest. A girl could hope, couldn't she?

The parking lot looked like the whole town was in attendance for the reception in remembrance of Edna. Caroline's back room would be packed. I squeezed my car into one of the last available spots. I got out and scurried to the passenger side to assist Mom. I warned her not to wear those heels, especially for the graveside service. That's all I needed. For her to end up topsy-turvy in front of all her friends. She insisted the shoes went with the dress and somehow we avoided the incident. She hoisted herself out with a grunt. I stood by in case I needed to catch her. I was relieved our route was a paved path leading to the store. We joined the flow of people funneling into Caroline's. There was a low rumble of under-the-breath conversations going on. I hadn't seen as many people in here since I'd returned to town. The same pitiful, sparse pastry display cried out for attention. Who knew how old those things were? Likely the amount of sugar preserved them for eternity. We all passed through the store into the meeting room. I spotted Buzz and Pearl to the side as we entered and gave a small wave and head nod. People milled about in an uncomfortable presence.

"Mom, I'm going to say hi to Buzz. Do you want to find a seat?"

She selected a table mid-room. A prime location to watch the show. I sat my purse in the chair next to her and wove my way through the bodies to reach Buzz.

"This is quite a turnout, huh?" I said.

"Yeah, it's nice," Buzz said. "Though I'm a bit skeptical that some people are just here for the gossip. Nonetheless, I'm glad to see it. How's your mom doing?"

I looked him in the eye. "Judging by the usual amount of tart to her comments? She's doing OK. I think it reminds her, and all of us, of our own mortality. And that's sobering."

"You got that right. Hey, we really need to get that golf game in. I don't care if you're rusty. It'll be fun."

I chuckled. "Rusty? That would be an improvement. Get ready for a triple-digit score."

He quietly snickered. "You know, even the guys I play with regularly have that issue. So you'll fit right in."

"OK everyone." Oddly, Caroline had a pretty huge grin on her face. "We're about to get started. If you'd like something to eat, you need to come into the store to buy that." I could see dollar signs in her eyes as she scanned the crowd, calculating probably the biggest boost to her business in a while. Not that she should provide the food free of charge. But I'd bet she offered her place so she'd get the business. I'd help her out. And the pastries, at least when fresh, were pretty good. I navigated back to the table with Mom to see that Brittany had joined her.

"Hi, Aunt Chloe."

"Hi, Britt. I'm going to get something to eat. Would either of you like something?"

"I'm not giving that woman a dime of my hard-earned money." I'd expect nothing less of a response from Mom.

"Yes, please," Brittany said. "And, Aunt Chloe. Do you know that guy who came late to the service? I didn't recognize him."

"Not sure, exactly. But I think it was the same guy who checked into the hotel yesterday. I mean, he looks a lot different. But I can't shake the feeling that there's something familiar about him."

"The person at the hotel had long hair, sloppy clothes. It wasn't him," Mom confidently said.

She would probably know. She had a keen eye for details if it had anything to do with the theater that was this town.

Loretta, overhearing our conversation, chimed in, "I saw him at the bank too." Seriously, there was no way you'd ever get away with anything in this town. They didn't need to find the budget for the town cop. They could just crowdsource the investigation and save a lot of money. "Maybe he's a lawyer. He's all fancy in that suit."

There was a familiarity about him. But probably our stressed brains playing tricks. Without knowing the real reason for Edna's death, speculation continued to abound. We needed answers, and fast. If much more time passed without clarity, we'd probably have a full-blown riot on our hands.

CHAPTER SIXTEEN

This was not going to be easy. Edna and Ralph's house looked like an antique store had exploded. Don't get me wrong, there were many beautiful pieces displayed in every room, on every surface. I partially reconsidered my volunteering to help Ralph sort through Edna's things. This would be tedious. But maybe I'd get some more answers to the outstanding questions around Edna's death. We'd need a strategy to get through this in a timely manner. The only possible family of Edna's that I knew of was the nephew mentioned by Ralph. First thing was we'd organize and inventory Edna's things. We decided we'd each take a room and tackle it, but we might need reinforcements. Ralph hauled in stacks of varying sized boxes and supplies to start packing.

I returned to the living room and planned to go through the paperwork on Edna's desk. Before I settled in, I let the pups outside to expend energy. I needed them calm while we went through Edna's things. I strolled around the beautiful garden while the dogs explored. They raced back and forth at top speed. We'd worked our way to the opposite end of the yard and were making the return trip. Passing by Edna's gnomes from the opposite angle as I had the other day, I noticed the missing gnome, *Speak No Evil*, had fallen under a bush. I grabbed it and returned it to its place next to *See No Evil, Hear No Evil.* I was ashamed that I'd even considered that Mom had stolen the gnome from Edna to complete her own collection. Even with all of her warts, she wasn't a thief.

I had to corral the dogs before there was any more damage. They panted with tongues out to the sides of their mouths. I found a couple of bowls in the kitchen and filled them with water. The slurping continued on for at least five minutes. Now I could focus on my task at hand. I grabbed a stack of papers from Edna's desk and sat on the couch. I began to separate them into piles. Bills to pay. Junk mail. Miscellaneous. I quickly completed that task and returned to her desk for round two. Max joined me in his normal puzzle-solving position, ready to dig in. Before we could access Edna's account to pay the bills, we'd have to speak with an attorney for guidance. At least I'd be prepared for that meeting with what we needed. I cracked open the book to see what I was dealing with. Nothing could be as messed up as the hotel books. I perused the entries until I got to those indicating she'd sent money to her supposed nephew, as Ralph had shared. It had been almost four months since she'd done that and every month prior there was a pretty significant amount. Her payments to the alleged nephew had continued to increase over time. Max placed his paw on the book, looked at me and raised an eyebrow. I needed another set of eyes on this to validate what I was seeing.

I traipsed down the hall to the bedroom, where Ralph was putting Edna's things into a box. "Ralph, question for you. I know you said Edna had been paying this guy who said he was her nephew."

"Yep. She finally cut him off a few months ago. That went on for too long, in my opinion. But it was her money."

"It looks from the entries over the last year or so that she'd increased the amount she was giving him."

"He kept giving her bigger sob stories. And she bought it."

"Why did she stop paying him?"

"You know, I'm not exactly sure. Maybe all of my badgering finally sunk in. When I first learned of it, she was extremely defensive and basically told me to butt out. It was none of my business. That was true."

I fanned myself with the bills. "Do you think she finally saw the light?"

"Yeah, she was stubborn." Ralph stuffed some shoes into the box. "It finally got to be her idea to cut him off. She told me after one of the final calls with him that she'd had it. He couldn't explain what he'd done with the money. It was always some BS story or another. I think it really hurt her that she'd been taken advantage of."

"Well, I'm glad she finally got to that point with him. You can't help someone who won't help themselves. No matter how heartbreaking their situation is." The bedroom was filled to the gills as the rest of the house, the dresser covered with every kind of jewelry. "Edna has some really beautiful pieces here."

"She sure does. I think most of it's costume jewelry and a couple of fine pieces."

The ring with the giant ruby looked suspiciously like the same one Mom claimed Edna's father had promised to her. I closed the book and returned to my tasks in the living room.

Trixie had assumed the dead bug position, her little snout snoring like a chain saw. Max preoccupied himself chewing on a piece of paper. That little rascal. I learned early on I had a canine paper shredder on my hands and took precautions to keep everything out of his reach. I went over retrieved the soggy paper. He clenched harder. "Max," I said softly. His eyebrows raised, still not releasing his prize. He shook his head *no*. "Max," I repeated. He slowly unclamped his jaw. I held the paper at the very edge, seeing that it was a receipt from the Emerald Hills Extended Stay Motel.

Where in the world did he discover this? It could only belong to Edna or Ralph. Did this confirm Ralph and Caroline were indeed having a tryst? I didn't want to believe it, but there was the evidence, right before my eyes. Poor Edna. I tucked the moist piece of paper into the books. I'd have to deal with that later. Again, more questions than answers. Was that nephew the real deal? On one hand I'd hate for that to be true and him to be the only living relative of Edna's who inherited her things. Especially after taking advantage of her. On the other hand, if she had no other family, I really wanted to make sure her things went to good homes. We'd have to see what the attorney said.

I found a blank notebook and began making a task list. *Another note to self: Be more organized with my stuff and directions for when I pass.* Being a widow with no kids, I didn't want any questions or extra stress about what my family was to do with my things. Especially my little buddy, Max. But we'd just have to hope my death wasn't soon enough where Max got left behind. And, for now, Trixie. Could I keep her too? Temporary custody was tolerable, but a permanent companion? I'd have to think long and hard about doing that to Max.

"Ralph," I hollered down the hallway.

He emerged from the bedroom.

"Yeah, Chloe? What is it?"

"I just got a call from Mom. I have to head back to the hotel. I'll check in with you later on next steps." He looked spent. I empathized deeply with him going through a loved one's things after they passed. When I had to do that with Frank's belongings, it was unbearable. Thankfully I had several friends who shared the burden. I was still pretty peeved at Ralph for his tryst with Caroline, though. I just hoped if they were going to advance their relationship, they'd wait an appropriate amount of time. I signaled the pups it was time to go. They jumped up and the race for the front seat was on. I was pretty sure if Trixie could talk I'd have heard her call shotgun. Max waited for the door to open, knowing he'd have no chance at the front seat.

I hated to lie to Ralph, but until I knew for sure I couldn't accuse anyone and destroy reputations. You never lived those down in this town.

CHAPTER SEVENTEEN

I picked up a bite to eat at the cute little drive-up burger joint, then arrived at the hotel only to find Brittany's car in the parking lot. I always hoped every time I drove up that there'd be more cars there of people who wanted to stay. The three of us piled out of the car and headed inside. I'd brought extra supplies for the pups to keep at the office since we were spending so much time there. They were treated as if they were the royal guests themselves.

I walked into the office. "Hi Britt. Hi Mom. We're back."

"How was it?" Mom asked. "Did you find out anything new? How is Ralph doing? I still don't trust him." She gave me the third degree as if I were a suspect.

"Whoa, Mom. Ralph is still pretty shaken, of course." I couldn't share any of Edna's business with her. No way I'd fuel the fire of gossip.

"Well, Buzz better call pretty quickly with an update. He promised I'd be the first to know." Mom demanded her due. Mabel was nothing if not always in the know.

"I'm sure he will." Little did she know, she might have a front row seat to more than she bargained for. I sat down to eat my lunch before all hell broke loose.

My phone started to vibrate and I saw Buzz's name on the caller ID. I'd called him after leaving Ralph's with my theory about Edna. He was pretty skeptical but said he'd check it out. There was really no other explanation for all of the clues I'd put together. I secretly think he was a bit embarrassed I got to that point before he did. Since his retirement, he'd lost a step.

"Who was that, Chloe?" Mom asked. Yep, right on cue.

"It was a friend from back home. I guess there was a storm last night and when she went to check on my house, a part of the fence was down."

She nodded, buying my lie.

Buzz warned me that we might be in the eye of the storm any minute. The call from my friend Cindy at the bank tipped me off that Arthur was trying to get into Edna's accounts.

Truth be told, I was pretty nervous after Buzz's call. I mean, could the nephew be dangerous? We didn't have anything to protect ourselves here. Although, setting Mom up with a gun had all kinds of disaster written all over it. Maybe a security system would better suit us. I attempted normalcy while continuing my lunch meal.

The door squeaked open. I jumped about a foot and almost choked on my burger. The clean-cut guy from the memorial service entered. He had all of his bags in hand. Brittany eyed me. *See, it was him!* Up close, I could definitely see it too.

I gave a small nod. I needed to act as normal as I could. "Can I help you?"

"Yes, I'm checking out." He placed his key on the desk.

"Thank you so much for staying. Will you be returning anytime soon? We have a discount for your second visit." I totally just made that up on the spot. I heard the faint sound of gravel crunching. Oh, please be Buzz. And please be someone with a gun in case this guy goes bonkers.

"No thanks. I won't be back."

There was nothing more I could do to delay. He turned and sped to the door like his hair was on fire. He opened it to greet Detective Jansen on the other side. I heard a squeal and a clap. I turned and gave Mom a look. This was serious. She continued to applaud like she was at a live show. Oh well. I'd let her have this. Better than a phone call from Buzz, it was a front row seat to the arrest. This would be gossip fodder for quite a while.

Detective Jansen stepped inside and grabbed Arthur's arm, turning it behind him to be cuffed. He dropped his bag from his other hand and the detective placed it in the second cuff.

"You're under arrest for the murder of Edna Gregory." Detective Jansen continued mirandizing him.

He led him out to his car and Buzz followed with the travel bag. The three of us went to the door to watch. The detective tucked the nephew's head and guided him into the back of his car. Already in the backseat of the detective's car was a man old enough to be Arthur's father.

"Why are there two of them?" Mom demanded. "What's going on? That's Walter!"

"Would you like to do the honors, Chloe?" Buzz asked.

Mom looked at me. "Chloe, what do you know about this? You mean you lied to me? And why is Walter being arrested? I mean, he was a terrible accountant. But, I didn't think it was anything illegal." She continued staring at me and waited for my answer.

"Mom, I didn't want to accuse someone if it wasn't factual. And in the end, you had a front row seat."

Appeased, she took a seat.

I could see the wheels turning in her head about how she was going to regale the Garden Club with the story. "When I was helping Ralph go through Edna's things I learned how Walter was blackmailing Edna.

I could tell from her records that she'd borrowed some money from the Garden Club one time but paid it back. She even pawned that ring you said Lloyd promised to you. Eventually, she must have turned things around financially because I saw the ring had returned to her bedroom dresser. Walter must have discovered she took the Garden Club money and was blackmailing her after she fired him. The embarrassment would have been horrific for her reputation. She cut him off and he must have been trying to get her to keep paying. He couldn't come to town because everyone knows him. So he sends his nephew, Arthur, to spy for him and figure out how to get into Edna's accounts."

"Chloe, I knew that hippie was bad business. Didn't I tell you that? And that horrible man, Walter. I'm pretty sure the only reason Sandy recommended him was because he's her cousin."

"Yes, you did Mom, but for a different reason. Anyway, I found a receipt at Edna's that was for the same place Arthur had been staying in Emerald Hills. Or, more accurately, Max found it. Arthur must have dropped it when he went over there. With Ralph having an alibi for that time, I knew he couldn't have killed Edna. Arthur may have just been planning to intimidate her but ending up hitting her with the gazing globe. Buzz told me they found a piece of it in her skull."

"I have to get on the phone to the Garden Club." Mom ran toward the phone. "They won't believe this. We might just have to have a special meeting so I can tell everyone what happened." Mom would ride this high for quite a while. She was already on the phone to Caroline. I hadn't seen her this pepped up in a while.

CHAPTER EIGHTEEN

Somehow, Mom had convinced Caroline to hold a special meeting of the Garden Club. It probably didn't take much persuasion. Everyone wanted to hear the details of the arrest. I suspected there might be some embellishments to the story, but this was Mom's moment. One of those times she loved being the center of attention. I was happy for her. If she enjoyed this, who was I to poop all over it? I'd vowed never to join a meeting again, but seeing Mom's performance was worth breaking my promise. The pups and I took our usual spot in the back of Caroline's meeting room. I wanted nothing to do with the spotlight. Caroline had even donated treats for the occasion. From generosity or an improved business plan? I wasn't sure. But she'd created a beautiful cupcake with a peony design on top. It looked as lovely as one of Edna's prize-winning flowers. For what seemed like hours, Mom regaled the crowd with the play-by-play of the takedown of Walter and his nephew, Arthur. She was quite the storyteller. How much more exciting and dire would it become with each telling? There wasn't much garden business going on, so Caroline gaveled the special meeting to a close.

Mom came to sit at my table. "Wow. My heart is still racing from the excitement of yesterday. A real-life criminal in our little town."

"Yeah. That was something all right. I'm so glad they got him. But why do people have to do that to others?" Having heard stories from Frank for decades as a police officer, I knew there was evil in the world. I'd never understand how you could hurt someone that way. "Buzz just called. He let me know that Ralph found a will in Edna's paperwork. Her things will be sold and a permanent scholarship set up for the agriculture students. Those blackmailing scum balls won't get a dime. Mom, we should probably get home to finish up getting everything ready for tonight."

Our family dinner had taken a far back seat to the murder. Mom wanted to return to the times in the past when all of her kids were together. Without Harrison, it wouldn't be the same. No chance he'd come for a visit while I was here. It might just have to be another time.

"Why are you worrying so much, Chloe? It'll all come together just fine. I mean, it has before. This will be no different."

"OK, Mom." We all got up and headed out to the car. I was still exhausted from the events of yesterday.

We settled into our seats for the ride home. "Chloe, I'm hoping Harrison can come for a visit soon. With you back in town I just need him for my family to be complete again."

Max gave me a knowing look. He really did sense all of my moods. I smiled warmly at my boy. His companionship meant the world to me. No expectations. Well, maybe some that had to do with ginger cookies. But he gave so much more than he took. If only I could do the same. I'd work on that. He was even generous in tolerating Trixie. No small feat.

"Maybe we'll try to arrange for another time." I hoped to appease her.

"Chloe, this is your home. And with Frank gone, you have nothing left there anymore. You need to come back. It would be so great if we could run the hotel together."

Maybe I will, Mom. Maybe I will.

＿ℓℓ＿

HEAR FROM MAX

Max tells his side of the story. Scan the QR code below with your device's camera to find out the scoop straight from the pooch's mouth.

NEXT RELEASE - VIOLETS AND VENGEANCE

C hloe and her mom are busy fixing up the adorable Buttercup Bungalow at the treehouse hotel when Chloe gets a disturbing call from her sister. It turns out Violet, the town environmentalist, has been found dead in the lobby of the local dog spa.

Violet's staunch environmental stance shouldn't have made her a target. But her constant protests and her questionable handling of the popular annual pet parade leaves Chloe with a seemingly endless number of suspects. A prominent town council member--and even Chloe's sister--top the list.

The shocking clues Chloe and Max discover lead them down a path that jeopardizes the future of the hotel. With the help of some huckleberry scrub, dog walks in the park, and her slightly overbearing mother, can Chloe and Max tie up loose ends and outmaneuver the killer to keep their beloved, quaint town from becoming a concrete jungle in ***Violets and Vengeance***?

Scan the QR code below with your device's camera to order now.

THANK YOU

Thank you for reading ***Peonies and Peril.*** Reviews are crucial for helping other readers discover new books to enjoy. If you want to share your love for this book, please leave a review for other readers. I'd really appreciate it!

Scan the QR code below with your device's camera to leave a review.

ABOUT THE AUTHOR

Sue Hollowell is a wife and empty nester with a lot of mom left over. Not far from her everyday thoughts are dreams of visiting tropical locations. She likes cake and the more frosting the better!

Scan the QR code below with your device's camera to follow her author page on Facebook.